THE
BELOVED
OF THE DAWN

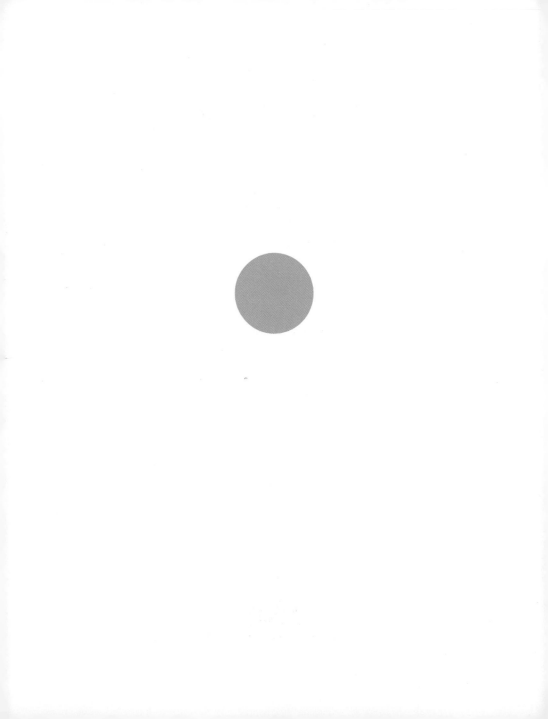

Franz Fühmann

THE
BELOVED
OF THE DAWN

TRANSLATED BY
ISABEL FARGO COLE

FEATURING DIGITAL COLLAGES
BY SUNANDINI BANERJEE

CALCUTTA LONDON NEW YORK

Seagull Books, 2022

Original German texts © Franz Fühmann, *Der Geliebte der Morgenröte*.
Hinstorff Verlag GmbH, Rostock

English translation © Isabel Fargo Cole, 2022
Digital collages © Sunandini Banerjee, 2022
This compilation © Seagull Books, 2022

ISBN   978 0 8574 2 900 1

British Library Cataloguing-in-Publication Data
A catalogue record for this book is available from the British Library

Typeset and designed by Sunandini Banerjee, Seagull Books
Printed and bound by Hyam Enterprises, Calcutta, India

CONTENTS

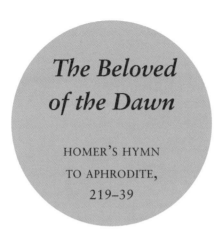

*The Beloved
of the Dawn*

HOMER'S HYMN
TO APHRODITE,
219–39

Eos, goddess of the dawn, once slept with Ares—every Rosy Fingered One sleeps with him once.

Aphrodite surprised them.

The act the two performed was consecrated to her; Ares, however, *belonged* to her.—She gave Eos a godsend of a curse: to want the love of mortal men so badly that the craving to surrender to them would outweigh that surrender's disgrace.

The curse was pronounced that very night, and Eos laughed it off.—Her husband was the Titan Astraios, she had borne him the morning star and the four winds who sweep the sea of air, and he sufficed her fully.—Ares was merely the inevitable exception, and that too would have sufficed for quite a while.—But as soon as the hour came for her to wake Day in his cave and show Night the way under the sea, on the way down from her peak she spied a sleeping shepherd under a fig tree in a field. Wrapped in a blanket he lay on his belly, legs drawn up slightly, face nestled in the crook of his elbow.

His helplessness touched her.

She couldn't resist slipping beneath him.

Calloused hands. Brown skin. Smell of sweat. Oh . . .

He dreamed and spent himself in his dream and woke a happy man in the red glow of the peaks: Eos blushing in the wake of her disgrace.

After rousing Day and ushering out Night, she shut herself in her chamber and bewept the twofold abasement: what had happened felt shameful and what was shameful felt sweet.— That night she goaded Astraios to satisfy her, and in the morning she chose a different path, and there was a different youth.— His parted lips, his defenceless chest.—A hunter; himself quarry; she lay down beside him.—Wine fumes and garlic, dried blood under the nails.—He woke bewildered, the mountains aglow.

Always a different man, morning after morning, a different impurity, a different tenderness.—Entrancingly imperfect beings, and always in a dream.—She avoided her husband, and he did not take it amiss: each found the other to be both cold and tiresomely importunate.—He began running errands to the stars, and on his way home he frequented the nymphs who lurked lustfully in the rushes on the Pineios, the Skamandros, the Nile, everywhere.

She never missed him.

More than once, when shame's torment grew too great, Eos set out to see Aphrodite and beg her to remove the curse, and each time she faltered and then stopped.—Curse as godsend.—For a long while she succeeded in slipping away as discreetly as she approached, until the morning she lay with Tithonos, one of the fifty Trojan princes born to the strong-loined King Tros.—Each prince dwelt in a chamber of his own; but Tithonos had a favourite brother Ganymede, of later renown, and between their rooms was nothing but a cloth partition.—Some say that they were twins.—When his brother moaned next door, Ganymede awoke with a start and came just in time to seize Eos as she fled.—He would let her go if she came back, next time to him.— What choice did she have?—She made her promise weeping the bitter tears of one caught *in flagrante*, and then she burned to fulfil it.—The brothers were brothers; without envy or spite they shared Dawn's desire. They pledged never to be enemies, nor to go near another woman so long as Eos was seeing them, and early each morning Eos slipped into their beds, Ganymede's today, Tithonos' tomorrow. Her shame had abated to amiability; she no longer felt like a thief, though she still had to steal about. The other brothers went unaware of her visits, but for the glow of her rosy flesh that gradually suffused the whole house.

The red of dawn at midnight—Astraios, running errands betwixt the spheres of dark firn, stopped in his tracks: there, on Asia's coast, between the mountains and the sea, was that an earthly star emerging? He reported it to Zeus, who looked down just as Ganymede was crossing the forecourt, doubly handsome in ecstatic expectation.—The god was staggered: there stood his ideal cupbearer!—As we know, he swooped down in the shape of an eagle and with gingerly claws snatched the youth away to the feasting hall of the palace on Olympus.—Painters see it in their own way; perhaps, between the peaks and the clouds, the frightened youth did lose control of his bladder, but surely it is false that he was still a child; he had killed lions and boars, and for half a summer had slaked the desire of the Dawn.

Who was disconsolate. Would that roving life begin anew?— But Tithonos did not disappoint her.—On through the autumn: peace each morning, and with it now the sweetness of the unshared and the prodigious discovery that even one single person can never be fully sounded. But there remained the self-reproach over the addiction to human love. For mortals are unclean creatures; they feed on sinews and blood, and their bodies channel faeces. True, now and then a male god must descend to sire heroes upon the human race, and goes uncompromised, being overcome by mere appetite. Goddesses meanwhile are sullied by mixing with mortals; yet: mortals love more ardently than gods, and their imperfection makes them desirable.—Their impurity too; it is a goad.—The brevity of their wretched lives concentrates their passions and makes them inventive in their enjoyment of the ephemeral: they are more tender than immortals. And they are constantly compelled to make sure of themselves, which is both touching and enchanting. And they find happiness only in that of the other.—No god would have kissed the down of her armpit when the small of her back arched. No immortal could so spend himself that his lust was, at the same time, ultimate surrender. Gods do not sacrifice to gods.

To spend eternity with Tithonos—but he was mortal.

To die with him—she was a goddess.—She desired this boon of Zeus: to fall asleep in Tithonos' arms and never wake again!—The lord over gods and men knit his brows in displeasure: that was beyond his power, and she knew it!—She knew: the Moirai themselves had decreed that immortality could not be revoked.

Then give him eternal life, that's a thing the gracious sisters allow!—She saw Ganymede in the ruler's chamber; he gazed past her, but she thought she saw him smile.—The moment passed.— She knelt before Zeus: Let me feed him ambrosia. Take from me the shame of loving mortals. Grant us what you have granted others!

Eternal life?

Yes: eternal life!

Let it be so . . .

And Zeus did one more thing: he sent Astraios far afield through the vault of the sky, thrice twelve years by human measure.—Eos took Tithonos into her home.—They were made for each other: thrice twelve human years of bliss.—In this space of time Helen was abducted, Troy fell, Agamemnon was slain, Odysseus returned to Penelope.—One of the sons whom Eos bore to Tithonos—Memnon, King of Aithiopia, lord of Susa's castle—fought for Troy, and Achilles sliced him open at the hip.—Tithonos, though a prince of Troy, had no part in the fighting. He never even learnt of his city's destruction, nor did he ever inquire about its fate. He lived with Eos, in her home beneath the roots of the sea. Nor did he weep for his son. He loved Dawn; that was work enough.

No mortal man; no trace of self-reproach, despite a few lingering imperfections. All the sweeter; and she too grew imperfect, sometimes letting her beloved distract her from her duties.—Some grumbled; Zeus indulged her.—On such a morning Day, abruptly blazing, would lurch straight up into Night, and mortals would stagger up out of their sleep; those were the hours of miscarriages and savage atrocities. On such a day the horses dragged Hektor behind them, Tithonos' nephew. Tithonos never knew.

Days without Dawn; and so too after that first midnight of frantic questions: What ailed him? What did he lack? What did he desire? Was he weary of her? Did he have eyes for another?—A siren? Hecate? A Nereid?—Dismal night, dismal morning, dismal day: What had faded his hair? What had wrinkled his skin? What had dimmed his eye?—A fact long since impalpably present, and long since impalpably sensed, abruptly revealed itself, and Eos understood: Tithonos had grown old. She had forgotten to obtain eternal youth to go with his eternal life.

And Zeus never grants a boon more than once in one matter.

Tithonos reached the age when mortals die. He did not die.— Astraios returned, journeyed off, returned.—Now she showed him Tithonos.

It was a funny little thing, she explained, she'd found it lying helpless on the shore, washed up by the sea, and taken it into her care. It had what seemed a sort of language, but no one could understand it: the squeaking of a mouse and the croaking of a raven. She commanded: Speak!—And Tithonos croaked-squeaked that he loved no one but Dawn.—She understood his cawing, Astraios did not. He laughed; Tithonos was allowed to stay on in a shed between the bedroom and the stall. And they, lovers again after such a long time, were vastly entertained at first.—Each morning Eos said: Dance! And Tithonos turned round and round. Astraios said: Show you're a man! And Tithonos exposed himself.

Sometimes she'd take him on her knee and scratch his bristly chin.

Time trickled on, a second Troy, a third, a fourth, a fifth, a sixth, and Tithonos lived on, shrivelled, gout-knotted, bleary-eyed, wizened, and each morning his impotent craving awoke. By night he lay nearly sleepless, waiting for stirrings next door; then he listened, his ear pressed to the thin wood: Dawn was getting out of bed.—She was walking to and fro.—She was washing, combing her hair, fastening her girdle, kissing Astraios.—He smelt her scent, he heard her voice, he felt her warmth, and he croaked-squeaked out his yearning: A kiss to start the day, he could still kiss, after all!—Astraios brought his food, ambrosia still.—Sometimes Eos came with him, and Tithonos would fall at her feet, sprawling across her rosy toes, and she would kick him away, and wouldn't come back until his morning whimpering became too much to bear.

Then he would lie at her feet again, small as a gnome, with a dry shrunken head.

Once Ganymede came to Astraios on some errand from Zeus, and when he saw his favourite brother, he took fright, and then he wept.

Tithonos no longer knew him.

Ganymede stood before Zeus again, eyes still damp: Take away his immortality! Though he knew it was impossible.—The Moirai allow mortals to take the step to turn immortal, but there is no turning back: one does not step away from immortality.

Eos ached with pity for Tithonos, but she too begged in vain.—Place him among the stars! she pleaded. Zeus gazed down, and said merely: *That thing?*

He did not ask whether she still loved him; that was not a question that arose among the gods.

No constellation, but a portent: from time to time, amid the gods' merriest mirth, or when they threatened to forget themselves, Zeus would show them Tithonos: This is the immortal mortal! Some of them shuddered, and some of them laughed, most brightly Apollo, purest of the gods.—His sister, Artemis, shrank from the sight.—And Tithonos, scabrous, claws digging into the wood, ears pressed to the wood, nose pressed to the wood, impotent sex pressed to the wood, croaked out his unquenchable yearning.

After a while they ceased to be amused.

The seventh Troy.

The eighth Troy.

They denied him food.

Tithonos dried up from within; the only moisture remaining was his spittle. As he clung to the wood it seeped from the corner of his mouth.—All that kept growing was his nails, and the howling of his hunger.—Now and then, through a hastily built hatch, Astraios shoved a dish of nectar into his shed.

Then his spittle began to stink, and the stench filtered through the wooden wall until at last it clung to Eos. Expose him on the hillside? Hades objected: He did not belong among the shades.— Move him to the palace? Unthinkable!—On the earth, in the sea:

no place would endure him, no rocky island, no mountain slope would take him.

Cast him into the water? The waves rebelled.

Putrid mornings; it grew unbearable. The stinking daybreak brought fever and plagues and, worse, confusion: mothers betrayed their children, brothers slaughtered each other, the host struck down his guest. Even among the gods pestilence began to spread.

At that Zeus went to see the Moirai.

They must alter their pronouncement, he begged, or fate would become snarled up in itself.—And the terrible, merciful sisters conceded: Tithonos could die; however, he would have to desire it.

But Tithonos was unwilling.

His voice was but a sigh, a mere sigh of immortality: He lived, it said. He loved Dawn. She would see: he still could kiss. And he would give her pleasure yet, if only she'd embrace him. All his trembling was only because she was avoiding him. Didn't she remember what he had been? His strength, his sweetness? Did she think all that could be over and done with?—And he invoked Aphrodite.

She appeared, she who alone never shuddered at Tithonos, nor laughed at him. She bent down and spoke to him, and he listened to her, and understood. And at last he consented: to lie once with Dawn, and, come morning, to perish in her kiss.

Stinking spittle; Eos shuddered. She turned away. She couldn't do it. And besides, it was time for Night to be escorted.

At that Aphrodite renewed her curse.

What Zeus did now was also forbidden, and yet the sisters condoned it.—He transformed Tithonos, the immortal, into a cicada, that gnomish race that each morning rubs together twig-thin thighs in ruttish bliss. And the cicada finds fulfilment: Eos every morning, the wafting of her saffron robe, her scent, her dew, her rosy fingers. And what had to happen, happened: Tithonos' voice turned sweet again, his body supple, his eyes gleaming golden, his heart full, his strength inexhaustible.

The ninth Troy, the tenth Troy, and cicada-song atop the rubble.

Up in the palace they like to listen too, Ganymede especially, and sometimes even the Moirai hear him. Then their grey faces brighten, and they move their icy hands.

There is just one who never hears him, and that is Dawn.— Aphrodite's curse hounds her, leaving her aware of one thing only: the body of a sleeping mortal. She lost all shame long ago, that heavenly whore, despised by all, in heat, indiscriminate sleeper with all, spurning not even half-grown boys. Each morning she slips into another's bed and flees again before he wakes. He dreams the rosiest dream of his life.—It is the hour when wishes come true, but let him beware immortality.

Hera and Zeus

HOMER'S ILIAD, XIV

What went before: beside the point.—By the tenth year Zeus had grown weary of slaughter, and decided to give the victory to Troy. Why to the city? Also beside the point; he was answerable to no one, but perhaps he recalled that the city, like him, was island-born. And there are rumours of a silken hand that caressed his beard, accompanied by entreaties; that may or may not be true, what counted was his will.—He seated himself on Mount Ida, the city to his right, the ships to his left, and ordered the gods embroiled right and left in the ranks of the mortals to quit the field and cede it to the fates that hover impassive, three terrible white-robed sisters, between the glaciers and the stars.—The Moirai were amenable to letting the divine ruler's will prevail, provided no other will vanquished his before evening came.—

Enough of the atrocities, enough of the confusion that by now robbed even the gods of their dignity; and to spite the most power-ful among them: Troy's victory!—Here on Mount Ida, where it had all begun with a cow-herding Trojan prince who had scorned Hera's favour and Athena's counsel and promised Aphrodite the apple of the fairest, here the work of discord should end, and the evening of this bloodiest day, whose very cockcrow was the shriek of iron, should be the armistice of Zeus' will.—He had commanded; the gods obeyed. They quit the battlefield, last of all Poseidon; with the voice of a thousand bulls he bellowed one last 'Hurrah!' to the men of the fleet as they pressed on towards the city, then hurled himself, resigned to rage, back into the sea. Hera, in the palace, saw him whirl down to the depths, saw the Greeks' assault falter, saw Zeus in Ida's grove, leaning back against a cliff in the shadow of the elms, his hands broad upon his knees.

'And so,' she said to Pallas Athena, 'this day of hope turns to carrion before eventide.'

Athena, obedient to her father, was silent. But Aphrodite, in her chamber, laughed as wild doves laugh, and laughing she saw the dust clouds surge back to the ships and away from the city of her prince.

'You are close to Zeus. He calls you little blue-eyes,' said Hera at last. 'Go to Ida and fall on your knees before him.'

Athena shook her head. 'No use. He wouldn't listen to me.'

'Try it.'

'Even this greatest closeness is fruitless.'

The goddesses looked at each other.—Inefficacy was indignity.—Athena said nothing to her father's wife, who was not her mother; she did not say: 'You are his wife!' She knew that Hera would merely laugh and show the scars on her wrists, by which, when she'd first rebelled against the ruler's will, Zeus had strung her up in golden fetters, an anvil bound to each foot, for three days and three nights above the abyss of the underworld.—Or the bite his scourge left on her shoulder, another time.—Or the heart's scars.—She dared not say: You are his wife! to her who of all divine and human wives was most often and most shamefully deceived.

Victory for Troy; it couldn't be helped.—Athena turned away, but Hera said: 'They are the people who tend our altars. They must not be left to rot in Asia!' She laid her hand on Athena's shoulder. 'I am his wife. Who else but I should go to him?'

Athena could not say: I will stand by you.

Even as the Close One withdrew, Hera cast off her robes and washed herself with the milk of immortality, called ambrosia, which nourishes the gods. She washed herself from her toes to her temples, omitting only her wrists and the swell of one shoulder.

Then she combed her hair and washed it and arranged it over brow and nape, draped herself in the robe Athena had woven for her, clasped it with a golden brooch and went to Aphrodite's chamber to ask her, Hera's foe, protectress of Troy, for the girdle of all-beguiling love to keep all day until evening.—The tale of how she succeeded has been told; the details are not important here: a bit of lying, a lot of flattery and faith in the naivety of the lovely one who with light hands casts the supplest snares but never imagines herself dangling in the snare of another. It was all that, and that the ruler's wife and sister so meekly came knocking on the door of one alien to her, the instigator of all adultery.— Hera got the girdle to keep till nightfall.—The poets describe it as vividly embroidered with the seven magics at work in it: pining, coaxing, toying, fondling, begging, yearning and tearful beseeching. But we know it was not so, it was a strip of undyed linen, and just as the seven heavenly hues merge in the white of light, so did all these magics converge as one epiphany: the certainty of being irresistible as the being that one is.—Clasping the girdle about her in front of the mirror, Hera had expected a change in her appearance befitting her young rival—whiter skin, daintier ears, finer brows, softer flesh—and in its absence, disappointed for one twitch of an eyelid at being nothing but herself, she was prepared to think she'd been deceived; but in that same moment, observing her own form, clear-eyed in her scheming hatred, she discovered, stunned, that she was Hera.—*She* was irresistible, for she was who she was.—Superfluously, that very same moment, her memory confirmed the girdle's authenticity: Aphrodite, having never before removed it, had worn it that long-ago time, that time branded into place, at the foot of Mount Ida, when the three of them stood before the Trojan: Pallas in her golden armour, the Wanton One with the strip of linen beneath her gauzy veil, and she in the blue robe now parted about her bosom. At that time she had wished in secret that that pink, the incomparable pink of Aphrodite's breasts were hers; now, though, the darker hue told her that the bosom filling the girdle was Hera's, a ruddier red, more sublime, shading into brown, and thus incomparable, for it was Hera's red and she, Hera, was the wife of Zeus, ruler over gods and men, who had chosen her for his own; no: she had chosen him!

She went to Zeus.

The poet tells us that she enlisted Sleep in her plan, a trickier matter; suffice it to say that she promised that shy, Zeus-fearing boy the object of his secret desire as his bride: Pasithea from her retinue, one of the Charites, three of Zeus' many daughters whose mother she was not.—Besides, she was wearing the girdle.—They strode across isles and bays; Sleep's tread soft as fog while Hera's feet made the land quake. No other goddess had a stride like hers; it throbbed with all the resilience of the ores, all the waving of the treetops, all the swelling of the sea winds. As she entered the forest of Mount Ida—Sleep, as a nightjar, alighted on an oak at its summit—Hector hurled the first torch at the Greek ships.—Noon's circle was full, its shadow still short.—Zeus, under the elms, by the cliff, saw Hera. She came from where he was looking, and down below the first deck blazed. Troy's army faced the ships.

All he saw was her.

Who was that being striding up, tall and radiant in the shade of the firs: his wife, or a newly arisen goddess of memory?—From what foam, from what sea?—Suddenly he heard all the springs of the mountain.—Who was that approaching?—Was that long-ago time returning after all: the night of his island, on Crete's Mount Ida, their wedding night, he in the shape of a cuckoo and she the One, the Unequalled, without whom his dominion meant nothing: Hera?—He stared at her; she came closer: Hera, the blaze of the Greek ships a mere glow upon her hair.—Her silent strides.—Blue robe.—Her eyes.—Now the brooch gleamed. Her bosom.

He asked where she was going, more brusquely than he meant to; she couldn't be going far, without horse and chariot; and she replied: To the end of the earth, to Father Okeanos and Mother Tethys, for the ancient couple's wedding anniversary. The same lie she'd told to Aphrodite, asking: Could a matron's face with its wrinkles and folds make her husband's passion flare once more?—A lie, but truth now that she told it to the ruler: If Zeus were to say *So go!*, she would go. She said the chariot was waiting at the mountain's foot, by the springs; that was nothing but a lie, all the more so as she pointed in that direction, almost the direction of Zeus' gaze, but he did not look down, all he saw was her.

Was that a bracelet on her wrist?

He meant to snarl at her, accuse her of coming to help the Greeks, but he said, he croaked out, how lovely she looked.—She accepted the compliment, obediently waiting.—She'd go now, she said quickly, just as he was rising up to seize her; from the palace she'd seen him sitting here and had come, as befitted a good wife, to tell him her intent and destination, and now she'd be off again, off to the earth's farthest bound.

The second ship in flames now.

'Stay!' he cried as she left the grove, and cried hoarsely threatening, and with that hoarse threat begging: 'Come!'

She strode on into the forest verge.

Her hair, and her nape, one swell of her shoulder, and her hands, and her whole form—no, not even that time when he'd wooed her on Crete, when she'd resisted him until he took the form of a tousled cuckoo hunted by cruel beaks, and fled between her breasts, and she lifted her arm to shield him, and he lay in the nest of her flesh, in the nest of her hair, in the nest of her scent: no, even then not so beguiling as now, about to vanish into the greenery.—That time he had ravished her, a cuckoo outgrowing its soft nest, three hundred years in human nights, for him one night only.—Hera, too, recalled the hour when the Mightiest One was so helpless that she could have smothered him: three hundred years a tousled cuckoo, even as he thought that he was overpowering her.—That night, three hundred years, he'd sworn fidelity: one night, but what a night!—He was Zeus, and he was who he was.—Then he'd deceived her ten thousand times: with her sister, with the Wanton One and with her retinue, with all the nymphs, all the Muses, all the Horae, all the Charites, with all the wives of all the gods and all the daughters of all the goddesses, even with his own, not to mention the countless mortals: she-humans, she-beasts, and even plants, and with boys, too, with monsters, with ghosts.—He was who he was, and now he was one who desired Hera and none other.

A few steps more.

Had he called out her name, that old, Cretan name: Dione, nymph of the oak tree, where the cuckoo and the dove nest? The Wanton One called herself by that name as well.

She turned around.

He, the ruler of the universe, rose.

She came walking towards him.—A walk without end.—The craving to see her unclothed—she whose body, he'd confessed even to mortals, surfeited him to the point of stupor—contorted his face and his voice.

She needn't worry that she'd keep the old folks waiting, he argued, and argued on, hastily, repeating himself, that it was only just noon, and evening far off; and then, abruptly: that she was lovely.—And then what she'd never heard from him since that time: she was Hera, she was the loveliest of them all.—And it's terribly true, and the poet describes it, that Zeus began to brag now that he was wooing, a bragging boy, defenceless against himself, shameless towards her.—She felt no hurt.—He stammered the names of her most fiercely hated foes among all those he'd deceived her with, mothers whose sons she relentlessly persecuted, he named name after name, and each time: 'You're lovelier than she!'

Tousled cuckoo.

She listened.

Lovelier than Danae, he stammered; wasn't that the one he'd come to as a golden rain, wasn't the brat called Perseus?—Lovelier than she.—Lovelier than Semele, he stammered, the one he'd pierced with a lightning bolt when, foolish thing, she'd followed Hera's dream-given counsel and made her paramour promise to appear in all his glory; he came in a blaze of lightning and thunder, and from her scorched womb emerged the most shameless one of all: Dionysus.—Lovelier than Semele; he said so.—Lovelier than Dia, who was she again? Oh yes, the wife of that Ixion who was bound to a wheel; she was some sort of shade now.—Lovelier than she.—Lovelier than Alcmene, mother of Herakles; lovelier than Europa, mother of Minos, queen of his isle of Crete; he'd come to her as a bull, and a part of the mortal world was named after her.—Lovelier than she.—Lovelier than Demeter, her sister.— Lovelier than Leto, ah, the mother of the twins, that other one who'd wanted to be queen consort and then was chased from isle to isle with that twin fruit in her womb in search of a place to give birth, and each island closed its shores, fearing Hera's wrath, until rocky, grassless Delos took pity and let her be delivered of Artemis and Apollo just as her belly was near bursting, Leto, wise enough to keep to the shadows now, the only one Hera was afraid of.

Lovelier than Leto?

Why was he silent?

'Hera!'—and now she was standing by the elms; not close enough; he refrained from reaching.—She asked what her husband wished; he found the words.—But if his desire moved him so, Hera replied, they must go to the palace, to her chambers with their roof and walls and the door so artfully fitted and bolted; it was not seemly here in plain view, on the open mountainside, beneath a sky pierced by gazes: she was his wife and not just anyone.

The brooch glittered; she was retreating; blue robe in the green gloom; he reached for her, wrist and shoulders, browner flesh, and her eyes were ox-eyes, large, brown, vaulted.—Her scent.— His wife: not just anyone; and he was Zeus! He stretched across the seas and snatched a cloud, pure gold when he touched it, a gleaming shield against all gazes when he pulled it over Mount Ida.—This, he said, would be their palace, the place where Zeus sojourned, and not even the sun would peer in.

Beneath the gold: her eyes, vaulted sky.

A linen girdle?

'Lovelier than Hera,' he stammered.

Triumphant cuckoo in her ruddy nest, in the flower nest that blossomed as the girdle's loops touched Mount Ida: crocus, hyacinth, lotus, a carpet, he raised her up, and Zeus was a mountain, and filled the valley.

Three hundred years?

The blink of an eye.

When Zeus entered her again, he squeezed the wrists he clutched in his fists; the mountain's weight bore down, and Hera knew that Zeus saw her now as she'd once hung on golden fetters, fetters of gold where his grip was, an anvil on each of her feet, he'd sat in front of her then and watched her face begin to twist.—Valley burying the mountain within it.—She knew he was remembering her most profound humiliation, which as a trial of his power had given him a different kind of pleasure: he'd been able to show who he was, and that in the circle of all the gods.— Did she regret having tested him?—All eyes upon her mute, defenceless torment, all the eyes of the bodies he'd deceived her with.—For three hours he'd sat in front of her, elbows planted broad on his broad knees, and he'd watched her, smiling, not even laughing, smiling, when even the dwellers of the underworld fell silent for pity and Hades began to sigh.—For a moment hate clenched her.—All the mountain's springs.—Zeus cried out.

Would they hear it down below?

Would Brother Poseidon glance up at Ida, see the golden cloud and grasp that his hour had come?—Had Athena told him of Hera's errand?—Had the fires been doused? Were new sails ruffling?

His back amid the gold: impenetrable cloud.

Even Hera's gaze could not cleave that shield.

How much time might have passed?

From noon to evening, say the poets; and one man who fought outside Troy and watched trembling as from the blue sky a cloud settled over Ida, shimmering like foam and dark like ore, and the springs of the mountainside surged all at once, only to run abruptly dry—one man knew it exactly: twice three hours, and at their midpoint the turning of the battle.

Zeus, lolling in the eternity-bliss of exhaustion, sought Hera's eyes once more: mirrors of the gold that was his power; mirrors of the lust that was his power; mirrors of the will that was his power.

Open.—His gaze in hers.

Vaulted eyes.

He kissed them.

A linen band; Zeus thrust it aside.—She, self-assured, noticed and did nothing; how else could it have been self-assurance?—Wasn't that a night bird taking flight outside?—His head sank down; she propped herself up.—And slowly, dimly, drifting off, he recalled: two snarled armies, a beach, a city, and victory to one side.—And he also recalled: it would come before nightfall.

What was the hour?

Golden cloud.

Dimly he guessed Hera's plan.

From the gold of the vault: her eyes.

Slowly Zeus thrust himself awake.

There she lay, face shuttered, the will that eternally crossed his, just as her gaze now broke through his again!—She who defied all his plans, eternally at work against him, in league with all the gods against him, the Crafty, the Scheming, the Cunning, the Shifty One, the eternal hounder of his nights, the eternal pitfall in the smoothness of the system, the eternal quarreller, the eternal nagger, enemy of his lust, enemy of his will, enemy of his sons, enemy of his lovers, enemy wife, enemy Hera . . .

Her white breasts' incomparable red.

Lovelier than all the others.

His.

Zeus knew he had to choose: his plan, or this moment, and she, reading his eyes, grasped that choice and what clinched it.

The girdle among the flowers: Did she pull it towards her?

He seized her hands.

Nothing but Hera.—Oh . . .

Mountain bursting the valley; and in the unfathomable self-exhaustion of the husband and the unfathomable self-surrender of the wife, it came to pass that even in this marriage beyond saving the miracle of their union was consummated anew: the two, eternally fettered together, merged of their free will in the melting breath of shared lust, which for a single heartbeat was love.—Each the other's bliss.—Each the other's slave.—Each the other's fate.—And Zeus forgot a second time, forgot the battle and the Trojans and the Greeks, forgot the ships and the wall, forgot the sisters' pronouncement, and she took the place of all he forgot, she, the Only, the Matchless, the Eternal One at his side, companion of his journeys, true counsel in confusion, point of his power, goad of his will, sharer in the fortunes of rulership, and again and again, in the eternal duel, that Other through whom alone each Self finds fruition. And Hera, too, forgot, and had forgotten back then, for one moment, yet for an eternity.—All the mountain's springs, all the valley's waters, and the battle in the distance: Hector by the sea.—He let go her hands and touched her hair, and drawing together amid bloom and gold they lay side by side, and he smiled, exhausted cuckoo, kissed the darker spot on her shoulder where the lash of his lightning had struck, and said: Lovelier than Hera!

And she: Mightier than Zeus!

My Dione.

My cuckoo.

Dione!

Cuckoo!

Very softly she called its call.—A nightjar cocked its head: a she-cuckoo beneath a golden cloud, and now, as Zeus sank into the meadow bloom, Sleep came, slipping through the cloud where the linen girdle touched the golden wall.

Drowsing cuckoo; Hera rose to her feet.

When Hera left it, the cloud was gold still, but no longer gold over bloom: a dome over a crater, dark and filled with thunder.

In the poet's telling, Sleep turned messenger for Hera and flew to Poseidon to call him to battle; others insist the opium-eyed boy never furnished such a service. Be that as it may, Poseidon appeared, hurling torrents down upon the burning ships, and his war cry woke in Patroklos, the hawk-bold, beloved of Achilles, the indomitable lust for battle. The particulars thereof, the Before and After and Meanwhile, is a long, sprawling tale, told in very different versions.—What we need to know is this: Patroklos, who with all the Myrmidons had been kept to the side-lines by Achilles' wrath, suddenly appeared on the battlefield and drove the Trojans back to the city.—Then he fell, to Hector.—When Zeus woke, it was evening, Hera was back at his side, without the girdle, the day-to-day following the night of nights, and the Greeks were swarming the walls of the city.

What followed then is quickly told: Zeus, in the boundless rage of a man who has thwarted his own plans, threatened to punish her as she'd never been punished before, but his wife responded that she had merely told him her errand, as was proper, and then, as was proper, set off, when his will had called her back; was there such a thing as a will opposing his?—So it was; Zeus remembered.— The Greeks raised ladders against the battlements.—Zeus frightened them off with a lightning bolt.

Then he went to the terrible sisters who dwell between the ice and the stars, silent, grey, and never forgetting.

The day was over, they pronounced, and pointed mutely down at the battlefield, where in the glow of moving torches the corpse of hawk-bold Patroklos swayed on the shoulders of the grieving victors.—There was no need for them to say it: the new snare. Now that Patroklos had fallen, it inevitably followed that Achilles would take to the field to kill Hector, who had killed his beloved Patroklos, a spear through his steaming entrails, and the death of Hector was the fall of Troy.—Resolved and vouched for: it was ineluctable.—For even the might of the mightiest is not almighty; they are caught in their own plans and the snares they create, like spiders in their own web.

Zeus returned to Olympus and summoned all the gods to the palace, even the lower gods, all the nereids and nymphs, even the deposed gods and the shades heard him speak.—It was his will, he said, that the battle should go on, not long, but long enough to consummate the glory of those whom glory should crown: Achilles and Hector. And then it was his will that by dint of the law of the Moirai the worthiest army should win.—And he took a golden set of scales, and laid in one dish the fate of the ship people, and in the other the fate of the Asiatic city.—So, he said, it was resolved that Troy should fall.—Hera bowed her head.—She sat next to Zeus at the golden table, and the gods heard the ruler's will.

And so it came that his will came to pass.

Marsyas

DIODORUS' BIBLIOTECA
HISTORICA, III.58–9

APOLLODORUS'
BIBLIOTHECA, I.4.2

For Heinrich Böll
17 October 1977

Marsyas was one who dared measure himself with Apollo in a contest, and with an instrument cursed by Athena.—He was a silenus.—His tale has often been painted and carved in stone, and a famous poet is thought to have made it the subject of a tragedy. Apart from that it has been lost, except where chroniclers tell it in their fashion.

The instrument was the double pipe, and Athena had invented it, it being in her nature to see the hidden potential of what is closest to hand. An alder twig, thick as a thumb; she hollowed it out and discerned as she did that the chamber would not be perfect until its resonance ranged from the depths of the nightingale's song to the heights of the lark's warble. That required two pipes; she joined them with one mouthpiece. The sound was sweet. Nymphs stepped out from the willows, and bellowing bulls fell still.

Athena hastened to the palace to treat the gods to the new mellow sound, but as the first notes rang out, Hera, the High One, began to laugh, and a moment later Aphrodite laughed too, and leaned across from her golden throne to Ares, who was yawning at her side, and whispered something so trenchant that he slapped his thighs and bellowed with laughter. Perplexed, still playing, Athena glanced at Hermes, who was listening with bowed head, but sensing her gaze he looked up, and seeing her he laughed as well.

Dumbfounded, Athena fled Olympus.

It was not like her to submit passively to insults.—Reflecting on her mishap, it soon struck her that Hermes had not laughed so long as he listened with eyes downcast. She hastened to the mirror of the nearest sea, and there she saw it: sputtering mouth, puffed cheeks, the veins at her temples swollen and blue. And suddenly she understood the snickering she'd heard, especially in Aphrodite's laugh: two male rods between her lips.

The virgin goddess hurled away the pipes with a disgust whose vehemence catapulted them straight across the Pontos to Phrygia. Athena sent a curse in their wake: whoever lifted this

instrument to his lips must refrain from approaching the Heavenly Ones, or else suffer a punishment crueller than laughter.

Then she washed her face in the salty sea waves.

Marsyas, roaming the beach, found the pipes.—We said that he was a silenus, descendent of the famous companion of Bakkhos, one of those shaggy, guileless creatures with the patience of a donkey, the trustfulness of a goat and the swaying gait conferred by a potbelly. They drink wine, sport hooves and long ears, and some, like Marsyas, have a bit of a tail. They are well-liked, even if they're sometimes found snoring in gardens. They are jolly drinking companions, seasoned night carousers—and now these pipes: wine filled the air! Marsyas played, and all of Phrygia, having fled into the mountain caves after Troy's sacking, crawled back into the daylight and started to dance.

Athena was nowhere near.

The pipes beckoned Cybele, the black-eyed goddess of Phrygian Ida, called Ammas by local farmers and blacksmiths. She appeared as a bare-breasted temple girl, reclined, drank wine, swayed to the notes and laughed, and it pleased her to remark that Marsyas played more beautifully than Apollo. The silenus was naive enough to heed her, and tipsily waving the pipes in the west wind, he issued a challenge to the god.

Who warned him in a dream: Marsyas saw himself wandering along the coast again, eyes raised to a sky so remote that only a flickering void could be seen, and as he strained his eyes to make out a sign, he stumbled over the pipes in the sand. He tried to pick them up, but they were too heavy to lift from the ground, and when he attempted it nonetheless, seizing them with both hands, his groin ruptured, and his entrails tumbled out.

All day long he shunned his instrument, but that evening brought back wine and warm contentment, and though Cybele did not reappear, the drinkers had not forgotten her words.—Flute-sweet moonlight.—More beautifully than Apollo! the gleeful cry went round the fire, and that night, after the silenus had once again challenged the god to a contest, he dreamed a second dream.

This time, again beneath an empty sky, a lyre appeared to him, descending slantwise from above, and when one string twitched like a bow, its sound was a whirring arrow that pierced Marsyas through his innards, from the navel to the tailbone.—Fright, and racking pain: the next day Marsyas stayed holed up in the reeds, and refused to come out when the enthusiasts called for him. Then it was the nymphs who begged, and when they brought wine, and bare breasts, and desired to dance their circles, he could resist no longer. He lifted the pipes to his lips, and they sang and sobbed out all the yearning that dwells in swamps. Marsyas grew drunk on his own music, most intensely when, afterwards in bed, he pondered it in the simplicity of bliss.

What sweetness; how could Apollo surpass it?

For the third time: Where was he?

Did he shy from the challenge?

Ah: the empty sky, and the lyre plunging!

Marsyas fell asleep. Apollo appeared.

All at once he was standing by the reeds with his lyre, his dark eyes resting on the silenus, who in tipsy surprise crawled out from his sleep, a bit dazed, and not even proud, pipes clutched in both hands. The god, on the gleaming gravel, against the green reeds, allowed not a single needless word, not a welcome. Marsyas offered him wine, and drank it alone, a few swallows before grasping that his opponent was waiting. With an effort he clambered to his hooves.

They agreed on the arrangements in the instant Apollo named them: one song each, beginning with Apollo, no spectators, for each the same conditions, the arena being the verge of Mount Ida's forest, and the tribunal being the Muses, those most skilled in speech and song, who go wherever Apollo goes, with the rest of his retinue, in the remote proximity tolerable to that commander of distance.

And the prize?

Apollo scrutinized him.

Marsyas never even noticed.—Meanwhile they were heading towards the mountain cloaked in morning's green, behind them the softly gurgling reed belt.—Scrutiny from between the roots; whispering ferns.—The silenus, not sensing Apollo's gaze, felt a thousand eyes upon him, companion of the Unapproachable One before whom all the gods of Olympus, but for Zeus, rise in respect—he to whom Marsyas had now gone so far as to propose that they agree upon a prize, at which a slight awkwardness crept back through his snugly mounting sense of pride.—A prize, as though they were heading for a festival where heroes gather to hurl spears or throw discuses or steer chariots around posts: Could Apollo possibly take it so seriously?—He was silent, apparently thinking it over.—Would he abandon the whole idea?—They strode along.—Marsyas feared the prize might be a golden goblet, which would merely garner him enviers in this reedy realm; the thought of losing barely occurred to him.—Perhaps it would be the pipes, ah, of course, the pipes!—Well, what of it!—He chortled: so that was what it was about!—But if he, Marsyas, were the victor, what should he claim?

Still Apollo was silent.

A skin of wine? Marsyas suggested.

He looked up to see Apollo looking at him.

The god declared that the prize would be no third thing; the vanquished would give himself into the hands of the victor to be dealt with as desired.

As desired?

As desired, and to measure.

Marsyas, striding on boldly, hooves clattering, scratched his belly.—As desired, and to measure!—now, that was a thought. It did sound a bit mysterious, but the first part sounded good for the victor and the last part not so bad for the vanquished.— Besides, the silenus had no doubts whatsoever.—He shouldered the pipes and laughed: Well, if he, Marsyas, won, Apollo would have to lug wineskins enough to fill a cave on Mount Ida, would that be too much?—Rattling gravel.—Marsyas chortled: A cave full of wine, the sweetest that grows on Samos, that would be a fitting measure, he'd accept no less than that!—They strode towards the mountainside, and as Apollo persisted in his silence: What if he, the god, did emerge the victor, what did he mean to do with Marsyas?

That he would learn, came the answer, and as Marsyas blithely speculated that he'd have to spend one lunar cycle playing for the Heavenly Ones on high, so that they, he giggled, so that they too might enjoy these sweetest of sounds, Apollo spoke: He would fathom him.

Him, Marsyas?

Him.

Fathom him?

Fathom him.

Wide-eyed wonder: How would that be done?

By fathoming, replied the god: He would seek the location of his soul, and, he added, which Marsyas did not understand, the seat of its hubris.

My soul sings from these pipes! the silenus laughed.

Cryptic words: Can emptiness be cleansed?

A confused whirring surge from the woods, and among the trunks, in the roundelays of light cast on the slopes through drifting clouds, the Nine Sisters, graceful of tread.

They stopped at the site of the contest.

The chroniclers relate its unfolding at tedious length and with dense digressions. Details differ between their accounts, but in essence all imply that the god won by means we can hardly call legitimate. For instance, that when the Muses, swept away by Marsyas' playing, burst out cheering and prepared to declare the Hooved One the victor, Apollo, thinking quickly, objected that the silenus had broken the rule that the same conditions held for both: Marsyas had used both lips and hands, while he, Apollo, had used only his hands, and now wished to move his lips; or, if that did not suit his opponent, let him use only his fingers. Whereupon, with Marsyas caught off guard and forced to concede the point, the god insisted on another concession: Thus far each had played just one side of his instrument, but the point was to demonstrate all sides, and so he would turn his lyre upside-down while the silenus must do the same with his pipes; and now, in the second round, to accompany his upside-down lyre, a song flowed from Apollo's lips in praise of the Muses, so pious, so panegyrical, so wise, that for them to grant the god the victory, they need hardly have heard the squawks the dunce brought forth from pipes held mouthpiece downwards.—Such were the tortuous attempts of the chroniclers to tease out a linear exposition from the interpenetration of opposing spheres, when in fact all that had happened was this: Apollo, with the vaulted cosmos as his lyre and a ray of the living sun as his plectrum, sang a hymn to that omni-potent light that is the pillar shaft of the day and the arrow shaft of the senses, a song that in praising the workings of heaven must of necessity praise the ones ordained to lend voice to those workings, the ones for whom thinking and being merges in song— that is, praised the Muses; and that following this divine work that sent tremors through the cosmos, a hooved, donkey-eared, potbellied fellow lifted to his lips a piece of bark filled with holes and let out something so unheard-of that the sisters felt, with an unfathomable shiver, how the very form of their language trembled

and cracked.—They, who grant words, had no words for what
happened, though it did happen, and happened in their hearing,
and happened to them: they could not comprehend it.—The
unheard-of.—For that emanation of a sweetness that melted the
senses was, with the god present, no longer that tranquillizing
delight with which Athena had soothed bulls, it was a thing cursed
by the goddess, and the Muses knew of the curse: they, workers
of tales, are those who know all that ever came to light, and
those to whom everything hidden in the depths is revealed.—To
think that one thing can be both: repellent and sweet, so sweet
perhaps because it was repellent.—The sweetness that beguiled
them was repellent sweetness, sweetness of the shunned, the
sullied, the unfitting, the downright unthinkable—epithets *ad
infinitum*, but all naming the ever-same essence of the ever-same
negation, an essence that has so many names precisely because it
is cast out from the Order and has no place there, but is there all
the same and, thus robbed of definition, becomes the Ungraspable,
harbouring universal form and threatening the contours of
Order.—Yet sweetness still; hence the shiver.—The temptation of
sacrilege, that was it, but merely felt, not yet put to words.—What
sang silenced those who were created to give speech: How then
could any choice be made?—There is no choice to be made against
one's own being, though that possibility, inconceivable sacrilege,
entices.—The saved and the cursed, cosmos and chaos, solid
ground and swamp, lyre and pipes, equal conditions of one single

contest, and the Muses, overwhelmed to the point of unspeakability, mutely gestured that the victory was Apollo's.—That was how it happened.— Marsyas, unsuspecting, bowed to the decision, at which the god waved his followers on from the darkness.

Cybele was nowhere near.

Wolf-light; two Scythians stepped from the depths of the woods, men of the north, they too followers of Apollo, holding catgut cords and knives with slender iron blades honed in glacial waters.

Marsyas watched them curiously as they approached with inaudible steps, and he still failed to understand even when they seized him, splayed his arms and legs, and bound him head-down, a shaggy Xi, between two black-trunked spruce trees.

The catgut cut into his joints.

But hanging head-down he couldn't play his pipes, he objected groaning.—He tried to laugh, and failed.—The pipes lay on the ground beneath his swinging skull; Apollo gestured towards them with one foot: So that was where his soul was hidden?

A jest! Marsyas protested.

Beneath his pelt?

All a jest!

Lightning flashing down.

Only as the Scythians began to slit his hide from the groin did Marsyas began to see, and at once his howls drowned everything.—He was immortal.

The Scythians peeled him out of his skin, first the legs, both sides, from the crotch: the thighs, the knees, the calves down to the bulging base of the hooves where leather merges with gristle.

Blood dripped into the howls of *Why*.

The incision from the groin to the armpits.

A whimpering for mercy.

Apollo: painters portray him watching, and striking the strings, and singing.—But none revealed how the victor devoured the sight. In his every look lies a solemnity that does not overflow, but contracts: the god tensed to the utmost degree still befitting heavenly nature, and overcoming his remoteness just far enough to let the one rendered into his hands comprehend his own howled questions.—He whom Apollo fathoms comes to know himself, within his own bounds and by his own measure, though this is not the reason why Apollo goes to work; he works from a different necessity.

We shall try to tell how it happened.

Even as they knotted him spread-eagled to the spruces, Marsyas went on thinking it a jest, a harsh jest in the manner of the Northerners with whom the Phrygians occasionally traded.

He took even the flash of the blades in fun: a tickle of fear to make him pipe the more sweetly.—The knife's entry was the incomprehensible thing: there was nothing he wouldn't have willingly done—play, wait at table, act the clown, all the things a silenus is made to do! He wanted to protest, explain, leap up, fall down, clutch the victor's knees, kiss the god's feet, offer himself with all that he owned, yet all he did was dangle twitching in the cords, and the avowal of his subservience was one howling drawn-out Why.

Apollo's lyre hurled it back.

Why?—the time for this question had passed, he was told; now the other one pertained: What is happening?—That dreary *Why* of his that the silenus incessantly howled out through the daylight—the time for that would have been when he stumbled across the pipes on the beach: Why they were lying there, and why so lost, and why as though they had dropped from the sky, and if someone had discarded them, why had they done so, and delivering what, blessing or curse? And when, desiring a contest, he had received warnings that even a silenus should understand, and felt clear forebodings in his kidneys and spleen, there would still have been time for a Why that might have altered what would come; but now that the god had appeared everything went back to one question: Why was Marsyas a silenus; or, meaning the same thing, why had he lost the contest?—What was that?—What was he mumbling, old wineskin that he was, amid his confused and indecisive howls? Might—here ended the cut to the bulge of the hoof, here the peeling began—might one gather that he knew everything now, that he understood, that he repented?

What?—Precisely, that was precisely it?

O what naivety: as though that were the point of the duel and that would put an end to it! Challenge a god and dismiss him again, as one picks up a piece of bark and tosses it away?—That wasn't it?—What then?—Guileless guilty silenus, even your repentance is the same as your hubris: one time you claimed you'd vanquish the god; this time you command him to desist! Ah, that old unchanged nature: Couldn't the silenus get out of his skin?

Up the arms, down the arms, and the blades slit through the hide of the shoulders and across the jaw and temples, then to follow the margin of the thinning hair and meet at an angle at the crown of the head.

After that they carved out the rump and the back.

The howling, having long since died to a whimper, moved down the throat, a dull dog-like thrum of the gullet, and as the lyre fell silent and the knives gouged the hide from the vertebrae, in their forest grottos the nymphs began to plead for the flayed victim, those lovely sisters of the satyrs and seleni who are also sisters to the Muses.

Woe to the flesh, the benevolent women wailed, must it always suffer for not being Spirit, and Marsyas unfit to measure up to

Apollo? Could these be duelling partners: silenus and god? Could such a naive, be-tailed creature even issue a challenge to a god like Apollo, and could the deity prove himself by forcing screams from the one so swiftly defeated? Oh, mercy on the flesh, poor guileless flesh; its pleasure was as fleeting as its sweetness, and testing it brought nothing but pain! Yet that pain could be wrought by rats and wasps as well, and even lice and thorns, and the dust! Did the Heavenly One wish to measure himself with these things? The howling gape of moist flesh—was this the offering fit for the purest of the pure? Were these cloying blood fumes a meal fit for his nostrils, this whimpering fare for his ears, this twitching of slippery fibres a feast for his eyes? The nymphs were not free to dispute, but they ventured to plead: He was the Heavenly One, the worker of healing—would not mercy befit him?

Whispered entreaties; they never showed themselves, but the moss breathed out their yearning.

What heals, fair sisters, is knowledge, but what matters is not whether Marsyas knows, and it is not his hide that needs to be healed.

Sighing woods.

The Muses listened.

By now the work had progressed so far that the occiput, the back, the rump and the legs—from the slant of the groin to the hooves—had been peeled free from their coat, but as the hide and the flesh were still joined at the hooves, the skin did not fall over Marsyas' head, which the kneeling Skythians now laid across their thighs to attend to the face.

At that moment the two gazes met: the silenus' and the god's.

The lyre said: The eyes of the spirit begin to see clearly only when the body's eyes blur. As the vanquished is now approaching that point, he might experience the onset of this clarity. Marsyas, it said, already saw more keenly now: saw himself and his opponent as not of one kind and not fit to be measured with one yardstick; to be sure, he recognized them only as the flayed and the flayer, and that insight did not penetrate either being deeply, but it did point the way.—Who Apollo was, Marsyas had no need to grasp, it was enough that the Muses should learn it; what the silenus was, would be shown to them, and, as his bodily eyes dimmed, perhaps even to Marsyas.

One Scythian clutched the sparse hank of hair, and they used their blades to loosen the skin, then pull it—along with the eyeballs and, a moment later, the gasping lips—down over the cheekbones and the chin.

The tongue in the bare, roaring gorge; the open gullet; the bellows of the lungs.

The nipples.

Fat and jelly.

The rod.

The hide had been shucked from the flesh, but the hooves still held the body together. The whimpering now rose from the wobbling belly fat, and the blades burrowed their way in. A long slice through the muscles: the inside of the flesh, the hopping heart, spleen, liver, stomach, the coiling bowels, black gall, the kidneys' honey-yellow shimmer, and—pale vault—the bones.

In the pouch of the stomach, or the pouch of the heart: Where was the seat of a silenus' soul, the guilt of his guilelessness?

The blades pierced the entrails, and now the Muses, the nymphs' sisters, began to sigh as well.

Had Apollo considered, they asked, that that thing writhing between the spruces could not die?

The Muses are those who have no right to make wishes, for they tell the tale of what comes to pass: of Zeus' will enforcing his omniscience. And this means they must be impartial.—Their compassion exceeded what was fitting.

Apollo's grace: patience.

The thing baring itself amid the spruces, sisters, has committed the sacrilege none can revoke: compelling the deity to reveal himself. For when this is done, it is done completely.—Semele's fate: she demanded that Zeus come in the fullness of his divinity; it was done, and she burned.—There are two forces only that can compel such a thing, and both are beyond measure: amorous desire, and naivety.

A wave of the hand: the blades paused.

The Muses ventured to remind him: Semele's desire had brought forth Dionysus, the god of wine and benevolent madness. But what would the silenus give birth to?

His soul, sisters, which we are seeking!

Another wave, the knives' dull grinding, now piercing the innermost of the insides, tubes of the entrails, capsules of the bones.

Red fountain, yellow-trickling ichor, blood, faeces, brain, bile, phlegm, marrow, urine.

Which stream bears your soul, silenus?

A third wave.

The Scythians clipped the gristle of the hooves, slumping slippery lumps, and as the body plunged down into the pelt, Cybele roared up through the woods. Dark tempest, and the pipes rang out, the nymphs cried with hundreds of voices, and the silenus' flesh settled into the skin, juices, fibres, fat, entrails, and the skin, swelling, gold-brown, lusty, began to sway to the music, pointed ears, stamping hooves, wobbling potbelly, bobbing tail stump, rod erect to the open sky, and the arms clasped the black spruces, and their swaying moved the mountain and the woods.

The pipes in their incomprehensible sweetness.

The Scythians lunged at the pelt, but the force of their blows made it sway all the more, and the cuts closed without a trace.

Apollo motioned them back into the darkness.

And then came something unbelievable, but the Muses saw it with their own eyes: Apollo, purest of the pure, touched the skin, with one tip of the finger, with the finger's outer husk, and the skin gaped at his touch, but this spot closed too.

The lord of the Delphic oracle uses neither speech nor silence: he signifies.—What had to be done had been done.—Cybele roared away, the sound of the woods died away, the sisters' roundelay whirled off into the dusk, and Apollo, reminding the tiding-tellers of another form equally fitting to his nature, trotted silently northward, a wolf, and between the spruces hung a bloody hide.

Then evening came, bringing the peace of those who are guileless and fat and dwell in caves and love wine and all sweetness that is not violence, not between peoples and not between bodies, and the nymphs stepped out from the trees, and fires burned by Ida's springs, and the pipes sobbed, and the skin danced, and Cybele appeared, her breasts bared.

Then Phrygia was conquered by haggard peoples with sinewy limbs, the Galatians, the Bithynians, the Syrians, the Romans, and men with knives appeared again, long, sharp, honed in glacial waters, and bodies were cut apart again, men's, women's, children's, old folks', even Marsyas' hide, again and again. Soldiers cut him in pieces to patch knapsacks and boots and wallets and shields, but as soon as they had passed onward, the leather joined back together, and when the soldiers rotted away in the ditches by the wayside, in the swamps, in the deserts, the imperishable rinds remained, gnawed by worms, picked at by birds, and gradually scattered across the globe.

And Marsyas, that indestructible skin? It's said that mutinous soldiers stole it and planted it as a banner of freedom on their city's forum, between the royal palace and the house of the elders, and made offerings to the Disembowelled One, as their peer and their patron, with the playing of pipes by the open fire, and naivety, and benevolent women. The city's name has been forgotten, but we know that it was then conquered and razed, and its inhabitants were hacked to pieces, and that the restorers of order kept the skin in the cave of Kelainai, and rebels absconded with it, rebels with haggard faces, but here the tale breaks off.— Nothing is left but the account of the chroniclers, told in their fashion, and the pictures of the painters, and the statues, and the scraps on the road, roaming and roaming, perhaps one day joining the sole of your shoe.

And the sweetness of the pipes, incomprehensible.

And the remembrance.

And the curse.

The Net of Hephaistos

HOMER'S ODYSSEY,
VIII.266–366

When Hephaistos learnt from the Sun-Steerer that his wife, Aphrodite, was betraying him with Ares, he resolved to spite her by killing the Strong One.—It did not pain him so much that it was his blood brother; rather that it was, yet again, one of the dumbest of the dumb.—Though he made no reply to the Radiant One now guiding his steeds over the island valley, his lips moved.—The Sun-Youth laughed to see the Lame One standing outside his workshop, propped on his crutches amid the bellows' hissing gusts. He knew what he was thinking; that was why he laughed.—How can you kill an immortal?

From his smithy, where passageways branch off to the metal veins and the volcanos' lava-swamps, Hephaistos went down into his mountain.—The island was Lemnos, the mountain Mosychlos, its summit ringed by pillars of fire.—They call Hephaistos a hobbler, and blame his mother Hera for hurling him from Olympus right after his birth, dismayed by the infant's puny appearance; but they do his exalted mother an injustice. The plunge to the powdery red ground of Lemnos shattered the child's hips and thighs, and the poorly knitted bones undeniably aggravated the divine body's debility, but quite apart from that the hobbling stemmed from an inward curvature of the soles and toes so severe that the toenails pointed towards the heels: the body digs its claws into the ground where it stands, and whenever decorum forbids it to do so, Hephaistos reverts to a ludicrous limp, especially in the chambers of the palace. Now and then, to amuse himself and Hephaistos' siblings while they feast, his father commands him to wait on them, and he shambles laboriously around the table carrying the inexhaustible golden jug that he crafted on his island soon after his expulsion. With it he purchased his return to the palace, ignoring the warnings of his only friend Prometheus, whom the High Ones had also cast out.—Among gods and humans he usually walks on crutches, or propped up by his journeymen; but underground, where matter transports him, he passes like fire through the densest substance and shakes the roots of the mountains.—Now, on receiving the Sun-Youth's tidings, he pressed on with such force that his island's mortal dwellers, frightened by the underground rumbles, fled the midday cool of their homes and ran out into the hot open fields.

The couple in his palace at the foot of Mount Olympus heard not a thing, nor did it cross their minds that the Sun-Steerer might have seen them.—Now the shadows began to lengthen again.— Would the Lame One come home that night? Ares asked; she smiled. He wouldn't be back so soon, she reassured him; on parting he'd spoken of crafting something no one up in the palace had ever seen the like of; sometimes he'd shut himself up for weeks in the smithy or in his chasms.—'A new weapon?' Ares instantly asked, recalling for a moment his favourite tribe, the Thracians, at loggerheads with the more powerful Scythians.—But she shrugged: 'What do we care?'

The palace, lying deep in the valley, sank into the twilight.

Hephaistos stopped beneath Phrygia's Tauros Mountains at a vein of metal whose like he'd seen nowhere else. It was one of a kind: purer than gold, brighter than silver, tougher than tin, harder than iron and more malleable than copper, and only this one vein; and he had known where to find it.—The sight of it lent his wrath the purpose that grows from recollection.—Over and over he had pondered what gift to make Aphrodite from this metal, finally picturing a chariot like the shell on the swell of sea-foam that had floated that loveliest of the lovely to Kythera, a construct of mere breath, a shine on a void, yet bearing her weight like a feather, in the water, on the earth and in the air. —Well, so much for that.—On his way he had pondered a snare that would lace together his brother's wrists and ankles, no death of the body, that was impossible, but the death of his bodily power, a paralysed, twisted lump of flesh recalling Hephaistos' feet, which the Lame One could roll through the palace halls to the gods' eternal laughter.—But how to force the Strong One into that position?— The trick required would be the true masterpiece, but such talent was not granted him; that was the remit of his half-brother Hermes, and Hephaistos did not even envy him for it. Not that he would have despised the trick, the less so as a work of the intellect, but his art's medium was matter, the elements of the universe with the precision of their laws—not souls in their unpredictability. He thought little of those beguiling intrigues that nimbly play with chance, circling a myriad of possible goals with a myriad of possible paths rather than beginning with the imperative of a cause and from it inexorably wringing the imperative of an effect that then would subjugate souls as well. Not a web of tricks serving as a snare, but a snare in which the trick inheres; and suddenly he had it: the net.—The snare made of many hundreds of snares, the trap undetectable above the bed, and the bait beneath it the Sea-Birthed One, and everything was calculable. If the trap's invisibility was a given, the bait was a given too, and with it the catch; the melding of the bodies was calculable, and the trick lay in the trap itself: the indestructibility and invisibility of its material.—The invisible thread as the thinnest but the toughest, the most unyielding thread—can such a thing be made, and how can it be made? That was the problem he had to solve; everything else proceeded from that.—It was a problem that fit Hephaistos, and yet it was not the whole of his problem.

He laid his hand on the pristine metal.

The beauty of its coldness and resiliency, and the force of the fire that conquers them both.

He melted off a handful of the material and once it had cooled began to rub it between the fingertips of his right hand while stretching it out with his left. When hot the metal had a ductility, when cool a hardness such as he had never before encountered, such as could arise only here, as the solar plexus of all metal veins between the heart of the earth and its diaphragm.—Soul of matter: his medium.—What he needed now was the finest of eyelets: a flake from a diamond, shot through by a sunbeam. For the larger eyelets he had drill bits of his own, down to the thickness of a hair. That night he forged a winch with an extra-long crank; in the morning, outside his workshop, he awaited the appearance of the Sun-Steerer, and the first ray of light pierced the diamond.— Hephaistos let his journeymen go home to their wives, with gifts of wine and roasted meat. Raucously they thanked him; the smith shut himself in. He hammered the eyelets to a rail at suitable intervals from finer to larger, blocked the metal up in a rock crevice behind the hottest of flames, and began drawing it through the eyelets. Before turning invisible, the thread began to sparkle, then the sparkle was but an airy sheen, like ravished aether, and this sheen lingered undetected; nothing visible but air, yet the air was smiling. Now Hephaistos summoned his journeymen; they saw nothing; then they seized it.—He ordered them to tear that nothingness to pieces; the winch creaked, so did their shoulder blades, but the nothingness bore up. Hephaistos pitched in; the crank broke.—The journeymen were sent home a second time, the door was closed a second time, and the Lame One knotted his net.

Ravishing nothingness: the material's strength seemed sheer beauty.—The smith, entranced, forgot the reason for it all. He kissed the net.

Then he went back home.

He travelled under the Aegean as far as the coast, then hobbled the rest of the way to his palace, on crutches of gold, the net a smile upon his shoulder.

Aphrodite received him outside his palace.

The sun was setting, she said, how could it be that his hair was aglow?

'The glow of my forge, dear wife!'

He sat down by the hearth; she set the table.

He'd been gone a long time; was his work going well?—He gave a mute nod.—She clapped her hands and laughed: She was glad to hear it, and she was waiting patiently, however much she missed him; he shouldn't worry about her: his work required his attention, so she wouldn't hold him back.

Smiling air.

The smith spent two nights in his palace and made no move towards Aphrodite but to bid her a courteous *Good night* and *Good day*. On the second morning, while she fed her doves as usual, he lounged in bed a while, contrary to his habit, then reached for the golden crutches that hung on the wall nearby.— She hurried in and handed them to him.—He took his cloak as well.—He had to go now, but he'd be back soon to make her the obeisance of a gift such as no immortal had seen before.

He stood in the sun, yet his hair had no glow. She told him so, and he laughed out loud: He missed his smithy, as she could see.— She saw, she replied.—The doves fluttered up at the clatter of approaching wheels.

The Sun-Youth peeked into the valley.

She and he by the gate: he gestured as though to embrace her; she, gesturing him to desist, turned away.—Cooing doves.—He hobbled off.

Reaching the coast, he sat down on the beach.

Ares: two nights spent waiting; he was voracious.—His very first embrace tripped the net; they noticed it only when it snared his elbow.—At once she understood.—The Strong One tried to tear the net, first with his hands, then with arms and legs, finally with his whole body raging. He kicked and shoved the Lovely One; she shrieked.

And so they lay still.

We shall not go into the details of how the couple began to thrash again, then finally lay calm, nor is it crucial how their limbs were arranged.—Crucial is the invisible thread's tug at Hephaistos' wrist, summoning him back: that was part of the trick of the material. It alerted the Lame One to every movement.

Shrieking doves.

The smith stepped into his bedchamber.

As he entered, on crutches, feet dragging behind him, he hoped for one heartbeat to find Aphrodite alone, though his hope could only be vain: a certain weight was required to release the device that held the net.—What met his gaze was Ares, his black curls, his back, hiding Aphrodite and seeming to grow straight from his heels, his heels and his even soles, his strong, arched, even soles, looming like a wall, and suddenly Hephaistos saw his net.—The smiling of his fire, invisibility visible, the unyieldingness of the strongest material as the beauty of many hundreds of links, and he saw that it was his masterpiece, and desired that all should see it!—He hobbled to the enormous copper gong across from his bed, whose din, when struck, reaches all the way to Poseidon's palace, and with his toes dug into the fill of the floor he began to strike it with both golden crutches, crying for Zeus to come, shouting for Hera to come, yelling for Athena to come, and Hestia, Demeter, Artemis, and Apollo and Poseidon and Hermes, howling for them all to come, all the immortals, to see what no eye had seen before, and his howling drowned in the din of the gong, and his crutches were bent out of shape.

Exhausted, he gazed over at the bed: she and he.

His wife and the Strong One.

The net invisible.

Even as he'd started yelling, even as he cried for his father and ruler, Hephaistos had realized that he'd deceived himself once more, thinking he could show the immortals his masterpiece: they would see only the couple.—It was too late now; a din filled the air.—They strode up: the father and ruler, thunder blustering ahead of him; Poseidon, whose tread shakes the earth; Apollo in resounding refulgence; Hermes with the swish of his winged shoes; and far behind a clattering and shuffling and already the lesser ones' bleats and baas and whinnies: fauns, sileni, satyrs, empusai, lamiae and goodness knows what other riff-raff.—No echo of any goddess' footsteps; Hephaistos' howls had warned them of the sight to which he summoned them, and they were deterred by a sense of shame that only Aphrodite would have scorned.

The door crashed open.

They stepped inside.

All this, and the rest, has been told many times: Demodokos, the master of tales renowned far and wide, sang it at the feast of the Phaiakian king to the accompaniment of his arched lyre, relating in detail the winged words the High Ones in Hephaistos' chamber saw fit to convey to one another; yet it is doubtful that we can rightly grasp these communications; our words cannot capture the Words of the gods.—We merely seek to intimate what the smith heard.

He heard the laughter even in the crash of the door, that ringing, drawn-out, insouciant laughter that is so fitting to the nature of the High Ones, overflowing as it does from the fullness of souls poised in serenity, and from the laughter laughing words loosed themselves: that it seemed the Lame One was able to catch the Swift One, and the Cripple contrived to apprehend the Strong-Limbed, showing that injustice was not rampant after all; and the Cripple, the Lame One, the Crooked-Soled, who without meaning to, or even knowing it, had unclenched his toes from the solid ground, and propped himself on his bent crutches, heard Apollo laughingly ask Hermes if he wouldn't like to switch with Ares now and take his turn with the Loveliest One, and again he heard the High Ones laugh, long, ringing, hearty laughter, and he heard Hermes laughingly assure Apollo that he'd gladly lie upon gold-glowing Aphrodite, even with all the gods and goddesses watching, even bound by bonds three times stronger than this net—which was trickily woven indeed—and again a wave of laughter roared out, and as Hephaistos realized that they all saw the net, but saw it as no more than a gratuitous little trick needed only by a cripple to compensate for his crippledom—as Hephaistos realized this, he realized that his work revealed only his shame, as all artworks bespeak nothing but the shame of their creators, their inability to be like the others, skilled as they are at nothing but art.

Now he struck up a lament.

Alas, that he'd been born, lamented the smith, alas, that his parents had thus conceived and formed him, with feet whose nails pointed towards the heels, and scrawny thighs and gimpy hips, an eternal laughingstock for his brother, the even-soled, the strong-thighed, the firm of hip, the stout of body, so resplendent in the strength of his limbs that even the Loveliest One could not resist him; and as Hephaistos bawled out these laments he realized, again too late, that he was merely bawling out his shame again, the ignominy of his crippledom as a praise song to the Strong

One.—Who, resting on his bed, resting on the Loveliest, heard himself and the Loveliest praised, and the Loveliest heard the praise of the Strong One, and felt the gaze of the men on her nakedness, and the Strong One felt the gazes of envy.—Shameless strength; shameless beauty.—They performed before her husband's eyes.

The laughter was beyond all measure; now the lesser ones had entered the hall, with lustful looks and avid animal lips, and Hephaistos' journeymen pressed forward too; the master recognized the smoke-raw croaks with which, between anvil and bellows, they yelled to each other of the feats they did in bed.

Now they were laughing too.

At that he rebelled.

Hephaistos stood propped on his crutches, hunched over, for his crutches were bent, but his words reared up to a height of outrage that none had ever ventured before: His father and ruler had swindled him, giving Hephaistos his adopted daughter in marriage and blinding him with her beauty; she was lovely indeed, but filled with evil desires, a she-dog who'd cavort with anyone, even this loathsome god of war, the most hated of the gods, for all that he had even soles; Hephaistos had been given a whore as a bride, but now her nature lay exposed; and the Lame One propped himself on the gong and pointed his crutch at her splayed body: Let her lie there in shame forever, she, the object of all men's amours. At that the gaze of his father and ruler fixed him, but the smith's gaze did not waver.—Zeus held his thunderbolt in his right hand; Hephaistos dug his toes into the floor fill, and swung his crutch, and out-screamed himself: Let them remain fettered forever, or let his father give back all the gifts that the swindled Hephaistos had given as a bride price—the thunderbolt Zeus was waving, the Golden Throne on which he reigned; the Golden Table at which he dined; the Golden Bed on which he rested. And now, as the laughter abruptly stopped, the smith felt between crutch and fingers the thread that linked his wrist to the couple, and smiled upon by his forge's fire, he thought a monstrous thought: Cast the net over all of them, even the One heralded by thunder, and bundle them all together, and tie them up on top of the she-dog, and simply walk away to be with his metals and lava-swamps, alone as he had always been, and make his works for himself alone, works bespeaking the disgrace of his otherness and loneliness.

He seized the thread.

At that Poseidon spoke.

We do not know whether he read Hephaistos' mind; surely not that precise train of thought, but he must have seen that the smith was standing freely, and raising his crutches, and perhaps he saw the thread as well.—And he'd watched the Loveliest One melt away.—He, the fatherly ruler's brother, refrained from declaring that it was unheard-of to demand back all the gifts that make the ruler a ruler, nor did he condemn Hephaistos' unseemly stance. He merely said what was called for in such a dispute: he offered to arbitrate between the parties to the actual quarrel, that is, between the Strong One and the Lame One, and the arbitrator took the side of the Lame One.—The Strong One, said Poseidon, must pay the Lame One a fine, as dictated by law and custom; this must be negotiated, and proper negotiations presupposed the Strong One's release; he, the Sea God, gave a guarantee, backed by all his immeasurable treasures, that Ares would ransom himself honestly—and Poseidon's gaze rested on Aphrodite, and Aphrodite rested under Ares, and as the crowd suddenly parted, the smith saw his monstrous thought realized, and, tightening the thread, he dropped his crutch and unclenched his toes, and with a black fire in his belly hobbled towards the smile above their bed.

One of his journeymen grinned at him.

As Hephaistos reached for the net to lift it, he was unsure how he'd decide, yet all had long since been decided.—It was not that, crouching down, he saw the Loveliest One up close, and the sight robbed him of his will; nor was it a remnant of brotherly love.—It was simply too late.—He should have stayed on Lemnos, following the advice of his friend Prometheus, who, like Hephaistos, had once been cast out from the palace and had sided with those who are the Others to those at the top.—It was too late now.—Ever since he had purchased his return to the top, with the inexhaustible golden jug, it was too late, and that return itself had been nothing but disgrace, and the jug nothing but a testimony to it.

'Release the net!' the sea-god ordered, and Hephaistos released the net.

The Strong One leaped up; he did not strike his brother down, but stormed off to his favourite tribe, the Thracians, to take their side in battle against the overwhelming force of the Scythians.— The gods departed, the riff-raff leading the way; Aphrodite went down to the shore, and the sea clasped her in its arms, and she rose smiling from the foam, shining in imperishable beauty.

Hephaistos went back to Lemnos. He hung the net in his workshop; the smile of the air joined the smile of the fire.—His journeymen turned up, laughing and telling, as always, of the feats they performed on their wives.—Hephaistos ordered them to fetch gold, lots of gold, and smelt it; he melted down his crutches too.— He stood at the anvil, toes dug into the ground.—Then he began work on a piece for himself alone.

Hardly had he outlined the form when his father and ruler sent an urgent command: from the net he should forge indestruc- tible fetters, clasps around a left and a right hand and a left and a right foot and a vise about the hips, and the smith melted down the net and made the handcuffs, and then, at his fatherly ruler's command, obedient to his fatherly ruler, he took those unyielding fetters and shackled his friend Prometheus to the Caucasus.

After that Zeus allowed him to complete his work.

Hephaistos built two golden women who support him in place of his crutches when he limps through the halls and chambers of the palace, his toes bent to his heels. They set their shoulders into his armpits, and he lays his arms around their hips, where the warmth of the forge dwells. Their breasts are like the breasts of the Loveliest One, and they smile her smile, but the Loveliest One is lovelier.—He no longer touches Aphrodite, though he lies beside her when he dwells in his palace, and at the Golden Table he sits by her side. From time to time his father and ruler orders him to wait at table without those golden bodies, and he shambles around the table holding the inexhaustible jug, followed by the laughter of the High Ones; and when he thinks of his net, the black fire in his belly flares up into his face. Then his father and ruler may leave off laughing and ask, full of solicitude: Won't his dear son, the artist Hephaistos, be merry with the Merry Ones in their merry round? And the High Ones laugh from the serene depths of their imperturbably poised souls, ringing, drawn-out, hearty laughter, and Hephaistos, shambling, laughs along with them.